HOME  ALONe3

A novelization by Todd Strasser
Based on the motion picture screenplay
written by John Hughes

SCHOLASTIC INC.

New York   Toronto   London   Auckland   Sydney

To Bill, Kristin, and Brett Beaupre
(no relation)

ISBN 0-590-95712-0

12 11 10 9 8 7 6 5 4 3 2 1   *7 8 9/9 0 1 2/0*

Cover and color insert designed by Joan Ferrigno

Printed in the U.S.A.

First Scholastic printing, December 1997

Prologue

Peter Beaupre sat in the driver's seat of the parked blue van and watched the white vapor of his breath curl slowly through the open window and out into the frigid air. It was a cold winter night in Chicago, and he was seriously annoyed.

He shouldn't have been in Chicago. He should have been on a plane to Hong Kong with a stolen Axus Defense Technologies microchip in his pocket.

A chip that was worth *ten million dollars*.

But due to a stupid mix-up at the San Francisco airport he was now sitting in this van outside a cab depot on a dark, dreary block lined with gloomy factories and warehouses.

In Chicago of all places. There was no place worse to be in the winter. And for Peter Beaupre, there was no place worse to be, period. The FBI had been after him for seven years. His luck couldn't last forever.

1

"Can't we get a little heat back here?" Earl Unger complained from the backseat.

"Running the engine might draw attention to us, Mr. Unger," Beaupre replied.

"Then how about closing the window at least?" Unger asked.

In the seat next to Beaupre, Alice Ribbons sighed irritably. Earl Unger was a large, solidly built man with thinning hair. When he kept his mouth closed, he was good for grunt work. When he opened his mouth, he was a nonstop pain.

"The windshield will steam up," Alice replied.

"Hey, look at that." Sitting next to Unger in the back, Burton Jernigan pointed out the window as a mangy rat scampered across the street and disappeared under the van.

"Disgusting!" Alice grumbled as a shiver ran through her.

In the back, Earl Unger had an idea. "You really don't like rats, huh?"

"I hate rats," Alice replied through clenched teeth.

"You know what they say about rats," Unger said, silently reaching forward. "They can get through any opening that's big enough for their heads."

Alice glanced nervously at the open window. Just then, Unger slid his fingers down her arm.

"Ahh!" Alice screamed. In a flash a knife ap-

2

peared in her hand and she twisted around, looking for the rat.

Unger laughed.

"Why you —" Alice angrily pointed the knife at him.

Peter Beaupre had had it. "That's enough!" he shouted. "Don't you idiots understand how serious this is? Not only have we lost a microchip worth ten million dollars, but if we don't find it, Mr. Chou will use us for shark bait."

"Mr. Chou's in Hong Kong," Unger scoffed. "He can't get us."

"Mr. Chou has people everywhere, you jerk," Alice snarled. "If he wants you dead, you're dead."

Unger quieted down. Soon, a dented yellow cab pulled up in front of the depot. Peter Beaupre checked a number on a pad on his lap. "That's the one, boys."

Unger and Jernigan got out of the van and started across the street. In the van, Alice turned to Beaupre.

"Why can't we get rid of those two idiots?" she whispered.

"We will soon enough," Peter Beaupre answered. "But not until we get that toy car and chip back. Until then, we'll need their muscle."

He and Alice watched as Unger and Jernigan cornered the cab driver. The driver looked frightened. The three of them exchanged some words, then Unger and Jernigan returned to the van and got in.

"What'd he say?" Beaupre asked.

"He took the old lady to Washington Street in North Devon Park," Jernigan said.

"House number?" Alice asked.

"He couldn't see it," Unger said. "But he said it's a big, old Tudor house on a short street. Dead end."

Peter Beaupre leveled his gaze at Alice. "You're sure the old lady has that toy car?"

"She has to," Alice answered. "She was the only one with a white bag like ours. She had to be the one we mixed up bags with."

Peter Beaupre looked over the seats at Unger and Jernigan. "What if there's more than one big, old Tudor on that block?"

"We'll know the one," Jernigan said. "It's got a Christmas tree at the end of the driveway, and the driveway ain't been plowed."

body that he could only see in a mirror. He went into the upstairs bathroom, then closed the bathroom door and locked it. Then he pulled the stool over and stood on it so he could see himself in the mirror.

Then he pulled down his long underwear and slowly turned around to look.

"Ahhhhhhhhh!" A scream tore out of Alex Pruitt's throat.

4

Peter Beaupre parked the van a few streets over. For a while, everyone was quiet. Beaupre considered the task ahead. They had to find that microchip. To do it, they were going to have to go through nineteen different houses without being caught.

And they were going to have to go through them fast because Mr. Chou was an impatient man.

"I'm cold," Earl Unger complained.

"You're *always* cold," Alice replied.

"Just so you know, I'm not wearing socks," Unger informed them. "I thought we were going to Hong Kong."

"You can suffer a brief discomfort," Alice said.

"Brief discomfort?" Unger repeated in disbelief. "Who flew coach from San Francisco to Chicago? Me and Jernigan. Who flew first class? You and Beaupre. Who ate poached salmon and caviar? You and Beaupre. Who ate cold lasagna? Jernigan and me."

"We're in a transitional period," Peter Beaupre said. "Things will get better when we start the next phase."

"When will that be?" asked Burton Jernigan.

"Tomorrow we'll set up a base of operations," Beaupre said. "We start going into the houses the day after tomorrow."

"Wait a minute," Earl Unger said. "You want us to break into houses in broad daylight?"

Alice Ribbons looked over the seat at him. "This is the suburbs, Mr. Unger. People come home at night to sleep. During the day they go to work and school."

"She's right," Peter Beaupre agreed. "Nobody's home around here during the day."

5

Alex was lying in bed with the covers pulled up to his chin and a thermometer poking out of his mouth. His mom was sitting on the edge of the bed, and his dad was standing beside her. Stan and Molly were hovering in the doorway.

"What's the diagnosis?" his father asked.

"Chicken pox," answered his mom.

"Excuse me," said Stan. "But with all due respect, I think this is just a scam to get out of doing his science project."

"This is none of your business, Stan," Mr. Pruitt replied curtly.

"If infectious disease in my home isn't any of my business, then what is?" Stan asked.

"Can I talk to your father alone, please?" Alex's mom asked irritably, then turned to her husband. "His body's covered with spots."

A nasty smile appeared on Molly's face. "Would that include the buttock region?"

"Shut up!" Alex sputtered, his face growing hot with embarrassment.

"Don't talk with the thermometer in your mouth, dear," Mrs. Pruitt said, then turned to her only daughter. "Stay out of this, Molly."

But now Stan was into it, too. He turned to his sister. "It must include the buttock region, Molly. I mean, would he flip out so bad if his duff *wasn't* plastered with swollen, red carbuncles?"

Alex clenched his fists. He wanted to *kill* his brother!

"Don't you two have anything better to do?" Mr. Pruitt grumbled.

The two oldest Pruitt children ignored their father.

"What could be better then discovering embarrassing facts about your little brother's diseased dumpster?" Molly asked.

Alex shut his eyes. He'd kill *her*, too!

"Leave, both of you!" Mrs. Pruitt commanded.

Stan and Molly backed away from the door, but not before Stan delivered one final blow. "This is great," he said with a chuckle. "If he scratches his chicken spots, we'll be able to call him Scar Butt."

Alex shut his eyes and fumed. *Kill!*

Then he felt his mother's lips press against his forehead. "Don't mind them, hon. I'll make you some soup."

"And I'll bring the TV up from the family room," added his dad.

His mom stood up and patted him on the head. "I'm so sorry you're sick, hon."

"Try not to scratch those things," said his dad.

Together they left the room.

Alex gazed sadly over at the cage where his pet white rat, Doris, was crawling around in the wood chips. There was nothing worse than being the youngest kid.

After putting their youngest son to bed, Jack and Karen Pruitt headed for their basement. They had a week's worth of laundry to fold — not to mention that the laundry room was one of the few places they could talk in private.

"So here's the big question," Mrs. Pruitt said to her husband. "Who is going to watch Alex while he stays home and recovers from the chicken pox?"

"How about your sister?" Mr. Pruitt asked. "Could she watch him?"

"That was my first thought, but she can't," Mrs. Pruitt replied. "She hasn't had the chicken pox. It's terrible when you get them as an adult. I hate to say this, but there really isn't a soul I can tell."

"There's Mrs. Hess," Mr. Pruitt suggested.

"She doesn't like kids," his wife said. "Alex wouldn't go for that. Besides," she joked, "he doesn't drink or smoke."

"What if it's an emergency?" Mr. Pruitt wondered.

"I'm sure she'd be willing to help," Mrs. Pruitt answered. "But I can't ask her to watch him all week."

"I suppose not," Mr. Pruitt agreed reluctantly.

"Do you *have* to go to Cleveland?" his wife asked.

"I'm going with my boss," Mr. Pruitt answered. "I don't think I should cancel. What about you? Is there any way you could work out of the house this week?"

"It's a bad time to try it," Mrs. Pruitt said. "We're in the middle of the postholiday rush. But I guess I'll have to stay home. I don't have any choice. If my boss fires me, that's life."

"There's one other option," Mr. Pruitt said. "Could you leave him home . . . alone?"

"Not a chance," Mrs. Pruitt replied firmly.

"Even if you're at your office just a few miles away?" Mr. Pruitt asked.

"Well . . . " Mrs. Pruitt seemed to waiver. "I guess if he was feeling okay, and I only had to go to the office to pick up a few things."

"Think about it," Mr. Pruitt said. "You have a beeper, a computer, and the phones. Mrs. Hess would be your emergency backup. And don't forget, it's not like we live in a dangerous neighborhood."

"You're right about that," Mrs. Pruitt agreed.

6

The next morning, Burton Jernigan and Earl Unger were up and about at dawn, setting up for the day's work.

Before they left the ranch house, Jernigan dressed himself in a telephone lineman's outfit, complete with tool belt and hard hat. The hard hat had a tiny camera mounted on the side of it. Secretly, Jernigan was rather pleased with his costume. He liked the way he looked in the rugged workman's attire.

While Jernigan perched atop a telephone pole and took aerial photos of the neighborhood, Unger completed an assignment he found particularly demeaning. Muttering to himself, he sneaked down an alley and into a backyard dog run. As quietly as possible, he slipped a leash onto the medium-sized brown mutt within, then dragged the mutt into the alley.

The blue van rolled down the alley and came to a stop beside Unger. With a sigh of disgust, he

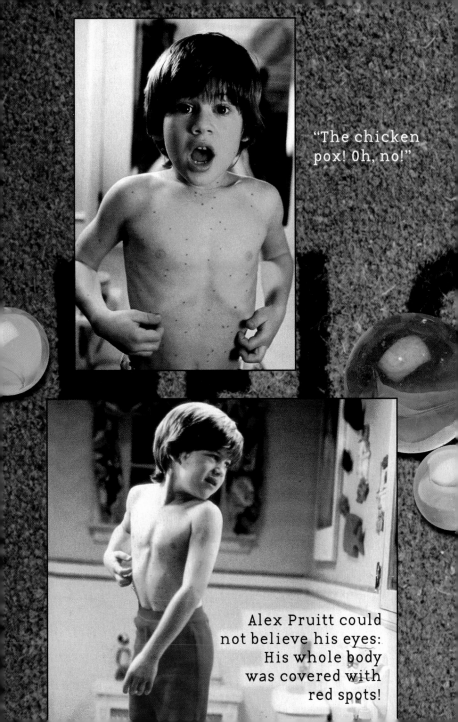

"The chicken pox! Oh, no!"

Alex Pruitt could not believe his eyes: His whole body was covered with red spots!

Alex began to itch while shoveling his neighbor's driveway. At first, he figured it was just his woolly winter clothes. Then, it turned out to be chicken pox!

Alex thought he'd get paid for his effort, but instead, all he got was a dumb remote control toy car.

Home from school, Alex was bored.
Then, his mom got called into
work and he was left home alone.

He looked through
his telescope and saw
burglars breaking into
his neighbors' house!

No one believed Alex! So he taped a video camera onto that remote toy car and sent it after the burglars for proof.

But soon, the burglars found the car, and were on to him!

Alex had to rig up traps to trick the burglars!

Soon, it was Alex against the bad guys— and Alex was winning! He hit them with a huge bag of plaster and a water balloon!

Uh-oh! The bad guys wanted revenge!

Alex found a microchip hidden in the toy car—so that's what the burglars were really after!

Alex had all sorts of tricks up his pajama sleeve to make sure the burglars wouldn't get away with anything.

Alex managed to keep two of the crooks covered in sticky plaster until the police got there.

He tripped up their female accomplice, too!

Because Alex outsmarted them, all the crooks went to jail—with chicken pox! Not bad for a kid left home alone!

So that was the whole gang of burglars.

Beaupre handed the toy car to Alice, the jogger lady. Alex's eyes widened with fear as Beaupre took out a gun with a silencer in it and went back into the house. Meanwhile, Alice pressed the toy car against her chest and started to peel the duct tape off the camera.

Alex smiled.

Maybe it wasn't too late to save the car.

Alex jammed the remote control forward. The toy car's knobby rubber tires spun against Alice's chest. The car shot upward and cracked her in the chin.

Alice reeled backward.

The toy car fell to the ground. This time on all four wheels! Alex quickly turned it around and aimed it out of the driveway.

The chase was on again!

Through the telescope, Alex watched Unger, the guy wearing the old man's clothes, race down the driveway after the toy car. At the same time, Jernigan jumped back in the blue van. For a second it looked like the toy car was going to lose them, but these burglars were pros. They spread out, blocking the street and the alley.

Well, it was a good thing it was an off-road vehicle. Alex turned the car and headed off across the lawns, through backyards, around trees and under shrubs. The four burglars went right after it, vaulting fences, crashing through hedges, diving over shrubs.

It was fun to watch. Burglars crashing into burglars. Burglars crashing into their own van. Meanwhile, Alex deftly maneuvered the toy car around to his own backyard, under his back porch and into a stairwell where he could open the basement door and grab it unseen.

With the toy car safely in his hands, Alex went back up to his room. Now all he had to do was take out the videotape, and show it to the police. Boy, would Stan and Molly be surprised.

He took the video camera off the car and hit the eject button. The camera opened.

But the tape was gone!

The burglars had already gotten it!

Filled with disappointment, Alex stared down at the camera.

Hey, wait a minute!

Disappointment became confusion. If the burglars had the tape, why'd they try so hard to catch the car?

Alex picked up the toy car and studied it. Sure it was nice and everything, but it wasn't that expensive, and those burglars didn't seem like the types who'd want to play with it.

Why would they be so eager to get it?

Alex turned it over.

Plink. A small square thing fell out of the car and landed on his desk. It was made of dark plastic. Thin strands of green and gold ran through it. Alex looked down at it. It sure looked fancy to be in a toy car. He looked under the toy car, but couldn't find the place where it was supposed to go.

He looked back at the chip again. Maybe *it wasn't* supposed to go in the car at all. Alex slid open his desk drawer and took out a magnifying glass.

He studied the intricate green and gold circuitry of the chip closely. He saw the serial number printed in faint red ink, along with the words: AXUS DEFENSE TECHNOLOGIES/U.S. AIR FORCE.

That *really* didn't seem like something that should have been in a toy.

Alex sat back in his chair and thought hard. He didn't know exactly what this thing was, but he had a feeling it was the kind of thing a bunch of burglars just might be looking for.

Well, now what?

He sure wasn't about to call the police again. They'd probably just laugh at him. Alex glanced down at the chip. What about the Air Force? After all, it was their chip.

Alex got up and went into his parents' bedroom.

How did you call the Air Force?

He started with information. They gave him a number. A man with a deep voice answered. Alex told him the whole story. When he was finished, he heard the man chuckle.

"Sorry, son. This is a recruiting office," the man said. "We don't handle matters like this. Why don't you put your mom on the phone and I'll refer her to the proper office."

Alex sighed. It was the same old story. Because he was a kid, nobody believed him. But he had to try. This was important.

"She's at work now," he told the man. "Can't you give me the number of someone who could help?"

"Phoney phone calls aren't funny, son," the man said, his tone getting more serious.

"I know that," Alex sputtered. "If you won't give me a number to call, can I at least give you the serial number on this chip? Then you can call the right guys for me."

"Well . . . " The man hesitated. "Okay, what the heck."

Alex picked up the magnifying glass and read the serial number on the chip to him.

"I really hope you're not just giving me lip service," he said when he was finished. "This could be really important."

"I'm sure," the man said.

Alex hung up the phone. There, at least he'd done his job as a responsible citizen. Too bad adults were such jerks!

25

The burglars sat in the living room of the ranch house tending their wounds. They had scrapes and black-and-blue marks. Unger had chipped a tooth from his collision with the van.

"I can't tell you how much I appreciate you hitting me with the van," he grumbled at Jernigan.

"You should have been paying more attention," Jernigan shot back.

"And *you* should have taken driver's ed," Unger snapped.

"Shut up, both of you," Beaupre growled angrily. This was a tense situation. Everything was going wrong. He looked at Alice. "What do you think?"

"I think we're dealing with a kid," she said. "It has to be a kid."

"You mean, because of how crudely the toy car with the camera was put together?" Beaupre asked.

Alice nodded. "The cops have come twice. Both times the kid tells them what he's seen, but they don't believe him. So what does he do? He takes matters into his own hands."

"It makes sense," Beaupre admitted.

"If that's the case, why take chances?" Unger asked. "I say tomorrow we whack every kid on the block. *Then* we look for the toy car."

The phone rang. Beaupre picked it up.

"Did you find the chip?" a gravelly foreign voice asked.

Beaupre swallowed. He didn't have to ask who it was. It was Mr. Chou.

"We're close," Beaupre replied.

"In other words, you don't have it." Mr. Chou sounded displeased.

"We will," Beaupre tried to assure him.

"Yes, you will," Mr. Chou agreed. "Because if I don't have that chip in twenty-four hours, the mission is terminated. And if the mission is terminated, so are you."

Click! Mr. Chou hung up.

Peter Beaupre put down the phone.

"Who was that?" Jernigan asked.

"Mr. Chou," Beaupre said. "We have twenty-four hours."

Unger grew pale. "What do we do?"

Beaupre turned to the map of Washington Street and pointed at one of the houses. "We hit this house. It's within the two hundred-yard operating radius of the receiver on the toy car *and* it's on the sight lines to all the houses we've been in."

"Whose house is it?" Jernigan asked.

Alice checked her computer screen. "It belongs to a family named Pruitt."

26

That night, Alex was allowed to join the family at dinner. Mrs. Pruitt slapped slices of pizza on paper plates, served the meal to her kids, and sat down.

"Now listen, kids," she said. "Dad will be home tomorrow night. I have my quarterly client meeting from lunch until five o'clock. I want Stan and Molly to come home right after school and stay with Alex."

Molly was the first to protest. "No way! I have gymnastics."

"I have hockey," Stan said.

"Do I have to repeat myself?" Mrs. Pruitt said with an aggravated sigh.

"I thought you were putting the bite on Mrs. Hess to watch Alex," Stan said.

"That makes a lot more sense, Mom," agreed Molly. "She's more responsible than Stan or me."

"She's just our backup," Mrs Pruitt explained.

"Unless it's an emergency, I'd rather not have to call her."

"Listen, guys, I'm fine by myself," Alex said.

"There you have it," Stan said with a nod. "It's settled. The twerp stays by himself."

"No, he doesn't," Mrs. Pruitt said in a tone that didn't invite any more argument. "You two work it out. I don't care how. But one of you has to come home after school."

"Great," Molly groaned. "As if this family wasn't fractious enough, now you pit me and Stan against each other for the sake of Blister Buns."

"Work it out," Mrs. Pruitt replied tersely. "End of conversation."

Stan just smirked and turned to his little brother. "Hey, Alex, could you pass the false alarms? Ooops! Sorry, I mean, the peas."

"Very funny," Alex said sourly.

"That subject is also closed, Stan," Mrs. Pruitt informed her oldest son.

"Hold on, Mom," Molly protested. "I respected your wish that we not pour any more salt into Pajama Man's copious wounds, but since Stan has inadvertently exhumed the subject, I respectfully request that I be allowed a last, final, farewell remark about Alex's law enforcement faux pas. I promise this remark will be amusing and warmhearted."

"All right," Mrs. Pruitt allowed. "One final remark and then we drop it forever."

Molly smiled and turned to Alex. "I just want you to know, dear little brother, that not everyone at school thinks you're an immature, attention-seeking, fraidy-cat, whiny-butt baby."

Alex narrowed his eyes and braced himself.

"It just so happens," his sister went on, "that the kindergartners think it's extremely cool that you got to meet the chief of police."

Another dig. Alex knew it was coming, even if his mother didn't. The phone rang. Mrs. Pruitt answered it. "Hello?"

Alex took the opportunity to shoot his sister a juicy wet raspberry.

"Alex?" his mom said into the phone. "Yes, he's been home with the chicken pox."

Alex looked over his shoulder at his mom, wondering who she was talking to.

"You live on which street?" his mom asked. She covered the phone with her hand and turned to Alex. "Do you know a Bradley Clovis?"

Bradley Clovis? The kid was a three-way dork. Alex gave his mom a cautious nod.

"His mother's on the phone," Mrs. Pruitt said. "Did you take a toy car from him?"

Toy car? Bradley Clovis? The realization of what was going on hit Alex like a slap in the face.

Meanwhile, his mom was talking into the phone again. "Yes, he has one of those remote control cars. . . . No, he got it from the woman across the stree —"

Alex leaped up from the table and lunged for the phone. He slammed his hand down on the hook and disconnected the call. His mother stared at him in shock, then pulled him away from the phone.

"What's the matter with you?" she asked.

"It was a lie," Alex gasped.

"I don't care," Mrs. Pruitt said. "You never disconnect one of my calls."

"I don't know who was on the phone," Alex said anxiously, "but you can't talk to her."

"Why not?" Mrs. Pruitt scowled.

Alex was just about to tell her about the burglars going into the Alcotts' house when out of the corner of his eye he saw his sister and brother watching and grinning. If he brought up the burglars again they'd ridicule him forever. Instead, he turned to the kitchen counter and took the school directory out of one of the drawers.

"Here," he said. "Call her back. I think you'll be surprised."

"Okay, I will," his mother said. But instead of looking up the Clovises' real phone number in the school directory, she punched that automatic callback feature.

Alex's jaw fell open. He started to protest, then remembered Molly and Stan. Meanwhile, his mom got back on the phone with "Mrs. Clovis."

"Oh, no, it wasn't your fault," Mrs. Pruitt said. "We're in the middle of renovating the house, and the phone lines are a mess."

His mom laughed at something "Mrs. Clovis" said. Alex could picture who was on the other end of the line. It had to be Alice, the jogger lady/burglar. Shaking his head wearily, he trudged out of the kitchen. It was too late.

Now the bad guys knew where he lived.

27

Later that night, Alex knocked on Stan's door and spoke to him. Then he knocked on Molly's door and went in.

Molly looked up from her desk. "Isn't there a law prohibiting a person from wearing the same pajamas for five days straight?"

Alex ignored her. "You don't have to come home tomorrow after school. I'll be fine."

"Gee, thanks," Molly answered with a droll smile. "Frankly, I was planning on sticking Stan with the unsavory task."

"You don't have to," Alex said. "I'll tell Mom you were here. I'll cover for you. I already talked to Stan. He agreed."

"Why?" Molly asked suspiciously. "What's in this for you?"

"For the first time in my life, nothing," Alex replied sadly and trudged out of the room.

*　*　*

Back in his room, Alex took his pet rat, Doris, out of her cage and stroked her gently on the back. It was obvious to him now that the burglars were going to come for him the next day after everyone left for school and work. No one was going to help him because no one believed him. Not his parents, or Molly, or Stan, or the police, or the Air Force.

Alex sighed and looked out into the dark. He was going to have to do it himself. He wasn't going to cry or feel sad or scared. He knew the burglars were grown-ups and criminals and a lot bigger and stronger than he was. But this was his neighborhood and his house.

And he wasn't going to let them beat him.

28

The renovation of his house had been a big pain, but now Alex was glad about it. Because it gave him all sorts of materials and supplies for the coming battle.

That night from the basement he got reels of wire, balls of yarn, and cans of spray paint. He found cable cutters, a fishing tackle box, jars of nuts and bolts, and a bunch of old weights.

He filled an old steamer trunk with books. He quietly drilled tiny holes in the front door and placed barbells on the roof over the front porch. He loosened bolts on the swimming pool diving board and slid a long, narrow wooden board under the pool cover.

He strung the thin, nearly invisible fishing line from his house to his neighbor's house, and then into the backyard. He crept into Stan's room while his brother was sleeping and stole his most prized possession — an ammo box filled with M-80s, cherry bombs, smoke bombs, fake vomit,

Chinese handcuffs, a hand buzzer, and a pea shooter.

And then there was the deal with the car battery, the jumper cables, and the metal lawn chair.

It took hours to set everything up. Fortunately the Pruitts' house was so old it was equipped with a dumbwaiter, a miniature elevator that worked on electricity. It wasn't made to carry people, but a small adult could squeeze inside if they wanted to. With the dumbwaiter Alex could move heavy things like the barbells and the books from the basement to the attic.

When he was finished, he crawled into bed and spread some balls of yarn, a small coil of fine wire, and a knitting bag around him.

The last thing he did was watch the weather channel.

That big storm was coming.

Alex's eyelids grew heavy. He yawned and slid under the covers. It was time to sleep.

29

At the regional bureau of the FBI in San Francisco, Bureau Director Albert Stuckey was just about to turn off his light and go home when his door opened and the young agent named Rogers came in with a sheet of paper. "This just came for you, sir. It's from the Air Force."

Stuckey took the sheet of paper. It was a fax about a child calling a recruiting office in Chicago about an Axus Defense microchip. He looked up at Rogers. "Did you read this?"

"Yes, sir." Rogers nodded stiffly.

"I know it concerns the stolen Axus chip," Stuckey said, "but it's from a kid."

"I think it's the serial number on the chip that piqued their interest, sir," Rogers replied.

Stuckey looked down at the fax and read the serial number the kid had given the recruiter. Then he looked through the folders on his desk until he found the report of the stolen chip. He compared the two serial numbers.

They were identical.

Son of a gun!

Stuckey looked up. "Are you married, Rogers?"

Agent Rogers scowled. "Yes, sir, why?"

"Because you're about to call your wife and tell her you won't be home tonight," Stuckey said, sliding the fax into the Axus Defense file.

"May I ask where I'll be, sir?" Rogers inquired.

"You'll be on a flight to Chicago with me," Stuckey replied.

30

The next morning, Alex sat by his window and watched Alice, wearing her jogging suit, come up the street walking the dog. The gang was starting its attack bright and early, just as he expected. He went over to his dresser and opened a drawer, pulling out a silver dog whistle.

Back at the window, he blew hard on the whistle. He couldn't hear the sound the whistle made, but the dog's ears instantly perked up. Alex smiled to himself. It worked.

He left his room and went into his parents' room. He could hear his mother in the shower. Molly and Stan had already left for school. Alex unplugged the phone jack and went back out.

Downstairs, he hid behind the living room curtain and watched Alice come up the walk and onto the front porch. She pushed the doorbell, but no one inside heard it because Alex had wired it into the phone lines.

Meanwhile, Alex blew the dog whistle.

The dog got up and came toward the living room.

Alex jumped up and dashed into the dining room where he blew the whistle again.

Now the dog trotted over to the dining room, making a loop with the leash around Alice's legs.

Alex repeated the process.

Now the leash looped twice around Alice's legs.

Alex smiled to himself. It was time to free the hostages. He snuck out the back of the house and around to the side of the porch. Alice was still standing there waiting, unaware that the dog leash was now looped twice around her ankles.

Alex blew as hard as he could on the dog whistle.

Woof! The dog barked and took off.

"Ahhhhh!" The leash went tight around Alice's feet.

Wham! She hit the porch floor and was dragged down the steps and through the shrubs by the excited dog. Finally he broke away from the leash, leaving Alice in a pile of snow at the far end of the driveway.

Alex dashed around the back of his house and inside, locking the door behind him. He went back to the living room window and peeked outside. Alice staggered to her feet and spit out a mouthful of pine needles. Her face was muddy, her hair was a mess, and her jogging suit was ripped.

Alex was fascinated by the elaborate concoction of cables and wires and electronic devices that poured out of one hole in her suit. He'd never seen anything so high-tech.

"Did you watch the weather for me like I asked?" his mother asked.

Alex spun around. His mom was coming down the stairs, dressed for work.

"Sure did, Mom," Alex said. "It shouldn't be a problem."

"Good." His mother went to the front closet.

"Wait, Mom, your coat's on the chair," Alex said.

"I want to wear my nice coat today," she said.

Alex couldn't let her open the closet. He dashed across the foyer and beat her to the closet door. "Why don't you go fill your commuter cup with yummy hot coffee," he said. "I'll bring your coat to you."

His mom stopped. "That's sweet, Alex. Thank you." She turned and headed for the kitchen.

Alex breathed a sigh of relief. He carefully opened the closet door, then jumped away as an old leather boxing glove shot out. He got his mother's good coat, then "reloaded" the closet and closed the door.

Alex brought the coat into the kitchen.

"Thanks, hon." His mom finished her coffee, then took the coat and pulled it on. Alex followed her to the back door. His mom kneeled down in front of him.

"Sweetheart, I'm so sorry about this week," she said, softly stroking his head. "It breaks my heart that I have to keep coming and going like this. It shouldn't be this way."

"It's okay," Alex said. "It's not you. It's the times."

"This is for you," his mom reached into her pocket and took out a beeper, which she clipped to his waist. "Promise me you'll wear it?"

"I will." Alex nodded.

"I'm going to call every half hour," Mrs. Pruitt said. "I'll go on-line with you and hold the connection open all day. I'll have my laptop with me in all my meetings. We'll be connected at all times. I'll also have my cell phone, and you know my fax number."

"We're wired," Alex said. But he knew she would get busy and distracted at work and probably forget to call. In fact, he *hoped* that would happen.

She kissed him. On the forehead, of course. And started to get up. Then she stopped. "Oh, my gosh! Did Mrs. Clovis call? She said she was going to come by before I left for work. She just wanted to make sure that Bradley's name wasn't on that car."

"She came while you were in the shower," Alex said.

"Did you give it to her?" his mom asked.

Alex nodded. "Big time."

"I hope she felt foolish," Mrs. Pruitt said.

"It was painful," Alex confirmed.

"Okay." His mom picked up her laptop computer and briefcase. "Be good. Be safe. And keep an eye on the old place."

"I have it all covered," Alex assured her.

31

Alex watched his mom head out toward the garage. It was starting to snow. She got into her car and started to back it down the driveway. At one point she stopped just to wave one last time at Alex. From inside the house, Alex blew her a kiss and watched her head off down Washington Street.

Then Alex stood alone in the kitchen and looked around. This was it. He was on his own. Unless you included Doris the rat and Stan's parrot.

For a moment he felt very alone and vulnerable. Through the kitchen window he could see his snow fort in the backyard. He wished he could just crawl inside it and hide. But he couldn't do that and protect his house. Besides, there was more work to be done.

On the front porch he hid a big puddle of marbles under the welcome mat. He stood some old ski poles on either side of the front steps and strung some yarn in between them. He hid a thin copper wire inside the yarn, then connected the end of the wire to an extension cord, which he plugged into an outlet.

In the backyard he set up Stan's trampoline under the attic dormer window and over the pool, and put some old Christmas trees on the pool cover. The snow was falling faster now and soon the whole pool cover would be blanketed. It would look like the trampoline was resting on solid ground.

Then he took some old snow and made the outline of a kidney-shaped pool somewhere else in the yard. He put pool furniture around it to make it look like a pool was there.

Next it was time to create his own headquarters. He set up the 8-millimeter video camera, as well as two older full-sized VHS models, and wired them all to old televisions in the attic. Now he had his own video security system monitoring all the entrances to the house.

Pretty good for an eight-year-old.

He waited for the burglars to arrive.

First a car pulled up and stopped in the alley behind Alex's house. Alex watched as two men got out. They were both wearing camouflage suits, but Alex still recognized them. One was Jernigan, the driver from the day before, the other was Unger, the one who'd pretended to be an old guy. Alex winced when he noticed that both guys were wearing ammo belts loaded with ammunition.

The other two burglars must have been on the move, too. Alex crossed to the other side of the attic and looked out the window and down at the street. There they were, walking up the street. Alice had changed out of her torn jogging outfit and was now dressed in a white snowmobile suit. Beaupre was wearing one, too, and carrying a briefcase.

Alex wondered what their plan was. Were they just going to walk up to the front door and knock?

Then he saw something he didn't want to see. It was old Mrs. Hess, coming out of her house wearing her housedress and thin sweater.

32

Peter Beaupre was delighted to see Mrs. Hess come out of her house. The timing couldn't have been better. There was no way they could take care of the Pruitt kid with that old bag sitting in her house across the street watching.

He nudged Alice with his elbow. "Look who's coming out to get the paper."

Alice smiled. "Shall we go say hello?"

"Definitely," Beaupre agreed.

They walked up to Mrs. Hess. The old lady had a sour look on her face. They would have to handle this carefully. They couldn't just grab the old hag and drag her back into her house. Who knew who might be watching. Instead they would simply have to be very persuasive.

"Good afternoon," Alice said.

Mrs. Hess looked at them and frowned.

"My husband and I just moved into the neighborhood," Alice said. "We're renting the Crays' house on Jefferson."

Mrs. Hess looked at her like she was crazy. "What do you want from me? A Wilkie button?"

Beaupre stepped forward. "We were supposed to have an important package delivered to us, ma'am. But apparently the driver got confused. We thought maybe he brought the package here, since you have the same address on Washington as we have on Jefferson."

"Nobody brought anything here," Mrs. Hess said.

"We checked with the delivery company," Beaupre said. "They told us no one was home so the driver left it in the garage."

Mrs. Hess shook her head. "Not *my* garage."

"It was the day before yesterday," Beaupre pressed on. "About the middle of the day. Were you home then?"

Mrs. Hess thought for a moment, then shook her head.

"My husband is an entomologist," Alice said. "The package contains several thousand deadly parasitic worms from Central America."

"They carry some dreadful diseases," Beaupre added. "It's really important that I find it."

Mrs. Hess rolled her eyes to make sure they caught her profound disgust. "All right. Come take a look. Let me open my garage for you."

Alice took Mrs. Hess gently by the arm as if to help her back up the driveway. Beaupre followed, lagging behind.

"Of all the people in the world, I have to marry a man who's interested in parasitic insects," Alice said with a wistful sigh. "My mother asked why it couldn't have been a nice lawyer or a policeman."

Beaupre lagged farther behind. He knew Alice would take care of the old lady.

Meanwhile, Alice and Mrs. Hess reached the garage. Mrs. Hess opened it, then turned around. "Where's your husband?"

"Oh, he had to go take care of something," Alice said, calmly pulling out a gun. "Make a noise and I'll make a louder one with this gun."

Mrs. Hess began to tremble. "Wha-what do you want me to do?"

"I want you to sit in that chair," Alice said, pointing with the gun at a lawn chair being stored for the winter in the garage.

Mrs. Hess obediently sat down. Alice took out some surgical tape and taped the old lady's mouth.

"Here's a thought for your next life," Alice said sweetly. "At airport security, always make sure you have the right package."

The old lady's forehead bunched up as she started to figure out what was going on. Meanwhile, Alice tied her arms and legs to the chair.

"Oh, and one other thing," Alice said. "I sure hope you weren't fond of the little Pruitt boy who lives across the street."

33

In the attic Alex had watched Beaupre and Alice head for Mrs. Hess.

Now what? He'd wondered as he watched them stop and talk to the old lady.

The conversation seemed to go on for a while with Mrs. Hess shaking her head and giving the two burglars suspicious looks. Alex couldn't imagine what kind of lines they were feeding her.

Finally Mrs. Hess seemed to change her mind. She led Alice up her driveway and let her look in her garage. Meanwhile Beaupre lagged behind, then changed direction and headed across the street toward Alex's house.

Alex remembered the other two burglars and quickly checked his TV screens. At that very moment, the guy in the driveway, Unger, was bending over the yarn Alex had strung. Unger had a pair of wire cutters in his hands. He was looking at a sign Alex had written and placed next to the yarn. The sign said:

WARNING! DANGER! HIGH-VOLTAGE
ELECTRICAL WIRE!
DON'T TOUCH OR YOU'LL GET ELECTROCUTED!

34

Earl Unger looked down at the sign, written in crayon in a child's handwriting. The kid was pretending that the yarn was high-voltage wire. Unger couldn't help smiling.

"Hey, Jernigan," he yelled to his partner, who was around the corner behind the house. "I think this is going to be fun. It's been a long time since I was a kid. I forgot how extraordinarily stupid they are."

In the backyard, Jernigan laughed. "You be careful," he called back. "Sometimes they wet their pants when they get scared."

"Right." Unger reached down and used the wire cutters to cut the yarn.

He didn't notice the thin copper wire leading from the extension cord.

ZAP! A huge blue spark burst around the wire cutters.

Unger's eyes bulged.

Thwack! The shock knocked him back and doubled him over.

Up in the attic, Alex smiled. That took care of Unger for a moment. Next he checked out Jernigan on the back terrace.

Burton Jernigan knew he might have to wait for a while. He noticed a metal lawn chair in the backyard and decided to sit. He was still chuckling about the kid as he dusted the snow off the seat and eased himself down into the chair.

Little did he know that under the snow the chair was connected to the car battery by the jumper cables.

Jernigan sat. Suddenly sparks started flying.

"Yeeeeeooooooow!" He let out a scream.

Bang! The ammo in his belt discharged, launching him out of the chair.

Wham! He flew face first into the wall.

As Peter Beaupre crossed the street toward Alex's house, he couldn't believe what he was witnessing. Earl Unger was doubled over in the driveway. His face was twitching, and the seat of his camouflage pants had been blown open by some kind of electric shock.

Around the corner of the house, Jernigan was on his hands and knees, looking dazed, and whimpering. Smoke was seeping out of holes in his camouflage outfit, and his mittens were smoldering.

Beaupre picked up his pace and hurried toward the house. He had to find out what was going on.

35

Knowing he'd bought a few seconds, Alex ran down to the basement and used a funnel to fill a balloon with water. He checked his watch when he was finished. It was about time for the burglars to make their next move. He went back up to the living room, pulled a footstool up to the front door, and watched through the peephole.

Unger had recovered from his shock. He was now standing halfway down the front walk. Suddenly he started to run toward the house, trying to build up speed before he jumped over the yarn Alex had strung between the ski poles.

Unger jumped. He cleared the yarn between the ski poles . . . and landed on the welcome mat with the marbles underneath.

"Whooops!" Unger flew up in the air.

Wham! He landed so hard on his back that inside the house Alex felt the floor shake.

Now Beaupre came running up the porch steps. Inside the house, Alex stayed by the front door watching through the peephole and listening. Beaupre looked down at Unger, who was lying on the porch, groaning.

"Mr. Unger!" he said. "What are you doing?"

"The kid's got the place booby-trapped," Unger groaned. "Don't touch the yarn. It's wired."

Through the peephole, Alex watched Beaupre cross the porch and pull the extension cord out of the plug. Then he went down the steps and knocked the ski poles aside.

Alex pressed his lips into a hard, straight line. Darn! That was one of his best tricks!

Beaupre returned to the porch and kicked the marbles away. "Have you tried the door?" he asked Unger.

"Not yet," Unger said.

"Let me point something out to you," said Beaupre.

On the other side of the door, Alex knew Beaupre had spotted the barbells he'd placed on the roof. Both Beaupre and Unger stepped out of the way so the barbells wouldn't fall on them.

Then Beaupre pointed at the fishing line Alex had tied to the door knocker. It must have looked obvious to them that the fishing line was the trip cord for the barbells.

Alex watched as Beaupre took out a knife and cut the line.

Both men kept their eyes trained on the barbells, waiting for them to fall. Neither man knew that the fishing line wasn't even tied to the barbells.

It was tied to the trunk full of books, hidden behind the dormer window in the attic.

Crash! The steamer trunk went right through the window and started to fall.

Unger and Beaupre looked up to see where the sound had come from.

What they saw was a large old steamer trunk plummeting down toward them.

WHOMP!

36

The snow was coming down hard now. As Alice left Mrs. Hess's garage and crossed the street to the kid's house, she was startled to see two bodies and a steamer trunk in the front yard covered with a thin layer of white.

Beaupre and Unger rose to their knees. Both of them were holding their heads. Both had nasty bumps where the trunk full of books had hit them.

"How did that happen?" Unger asked groggily.

"I don't know," replied Beaupre. "But that's it. I'm going in there and getting that kid."

"I'm right with you," said Unger.

The two men staggered to their feet and dusted off the snow. Then they started up the steps.

Upstairs, Alex cut the line holding the barbells.

Downstairs, Unger and Beaupre never even saw them coming.

Clang!

A sudden gust of snow cut off Alice's vision. She didn't see Beaupre and Unger climb the steps. She didn't see the barbells sail off the roof and smash them in the heads. Now Beaupre and Unger were on the ground again, holding their heads.

Scattered around them were books and iron weights. Alice walked up and stopped.

"You got hit by a book?" she asked Unger in disbelief.

"*Books*," Unger corrected her angrily. "Plural. A whole trunk full of books. And then a set of weights. We got hit twice, you bimbo."

"Excuse me, Mr. Unger," Alice huffed. "But I didn't get taken down by an infant. *You* did."

Beaupre sat up, holding his throbbing head. "We didn't anticipate the defense the boy would mount. We're going to have to presume that we're on equal ground with him and adjust our plan accordingly."

"I say we just burn the house down," Unger muttered.

"What about the chip, moron?" Alice asked.

"You want to know what you can do with that chip?" Unger asked angrily.

"May we continue, please?" Beaupre interrupted. "I'll go in the front. Mr. Unger, you take the north side. Alice, you take the south side. And let me know when you get that kid. I owe him one."

101

37

Inside the house, Alex couldn't hear exactly what the burglars were saying. But they didn't sound happy.

The three burglars split up. Alex knew they were going to try to get into the house now. He heard the front door knob turn and knew Beaupre was trying to pick the lock. Alex knew he might succeed in picking it, but he'd still never get through the front door. Alex had used wood screws to screw it shut.

The windows were another problem. Alex heard a sound coming from the living room. Unger had jimmied open a window. Now he was sliding a knife blade between the shutters to open the latch that held them closed.

Alex crawled under the living room table. Above him was a giant slingshot made out of bungee cords and strung from wall to wall. In the sling was a five-pound bag of plaster and the large water balloon he'd just filled.

Unger tipped the latch and spread the shutters. He stuck his head through the window and into the room.

Alex fired the giant slingshot.

POW! The water balloon and bag of plaster smashed into Unger's face, leaving a large white cloud. Unger flew backward into the yard and landed on his back in the snow.

Thump! Alex heard a dull thud coming from the vestibule. He grabbed a can of black spray paint and ran to the front door just as the mail slot flipped open.

On the other side of the door, Beaupre was trying to look into the house through the mail slot. Alex aimed the can of black spray paint at the slot and fired.

"Ahhhhhhhhh!" Beaupre lurched backward with his hands over the black stripe across his eyes.

Instant raccoon.

Next a jangling sound caught Alex's attention. Someone was trying to get through the gate from the alley into the backyard. Alex ran to the back of the house just in time to see Alice climb over the gate.

Bad idea, Alex thought with a smile.

On the other side of the gate was a muddy patch of ground. The night before, Alex had hooked a garden hose to the hot water line in the basement and run it out to the gate. Hot water had been seeping into the ground all night.

Splat! Alice dropped down on the other side of the gate and immediately sank down in mud up to her knees.

And somewhere in that mud was a trip wire made of fishing line. The line was connected to a cinder block carefully balanced on the roof gutter. When Alice hit the trip line, it made the cinder block tip out of the gutter.

Bonk! Alice collapsed into the mud. Now she had a nasty bump on her head, too.

With those three temporarily out of commission, Alex began to wonder about Jernigan. He hadn't seen or heard from him since he sat down in the "electric chair."

Creak! Alex heard the sound of the garage door opening. Now he knew where Jernigan was. He ran to the kitchen and peeked out through the window as Jernigan carefully stepped into the garage.

Alex smiled to himself. In the back of the garage was a loft. Alex had taken a big old stuffed gorilla of Molly's and dressed him in pants and shoes and put him up there with his legs hanging over the loft edge. The gorilla doll was part of a pair — one boy and one girl. For as long as Alex could remember, they'd always been together. Alex had hated to separate them, but duty called.

38

This was it, Jernigan thought. He could practically *smell* the kid in the garage.

There! From the garage floor he could see the kid's legs hanging over the edge of the loft.

"I got him!" Jernigan yelled gleefully as he reached up and grabbed the legs.

He pulled them as hard as he could.

Down came the kid.

No, wait! It wasn't the kid! It was an old stuffed monkey in kids' clothes.

And around the monkey's neck was some kind of rope.

It looked to Jernigan like a pull cord to a lawn mover.

Now, why would that be tied around the monkey's neck? Jernigan wondered.

Varrroooom! He heard a sound like a lawn mower starting.

Jernigan scratched his head. It sounded like

the lawn mower was up in the loft. But why would anyone put a lawn mower up there?

The lawn mower rolled forward. Jernigan looked up just as it rolled out of the loft.

Onto him.

39

"*Ahhhhhhh!*" came the scream. It sounded to Alex like Jernigan had just found out what it was like to get a close haircut with a lawn mower.

It was time to go up to the attic. Alex would have preferred keeping the burglars out of the house, but he knew that probably wasn't possible.

So he'd booby-trapped the *inside* of the house as well.

In the attic he turned up the volume on the baby monitor he'd brought up from his bedroom. The other monitor was strategically placed down in the living room.

Alex heard a sawing sound and assumed that Beaupre was now sawing through the front door. He had to say *one* thing for these burglars — they sure were determined.

The front door creaked. Alex knew Beaupre had gotten into the house. What Beaupre didn't know was that the front door was attached by a string to Molly's old Baby Sniffles doll in the front closet. The string pulled the loop in the doll's back that made sounds.

"Ha-choo." Through the baby monitor came the sound of Baby Sniffles sneezing in the closet. Alex assumed Beaupre must've heard it.

Thinking it was Alex who had sneezed, Beaupre would position himself in front of the closet.

He'd swing open the door.

"Uhhhhhnnn!" Beaupre let out a groan as the boxing glove shot out of the closet and hit him right in the stomach.

Bang! The sound of a gun firing caught Alex by surprise. Was Beaupre dumb enough to try and shoot the boxing glove?

On second thought, maybe the gun had discharged accidentally.

Alex checked the TVs. Jernigan, now sporting a flattop haircut that had sheared straight through his hat, had taken a ladder from the garage and was trying to climb into a second-floor window.

Too bad they were still doing renovations on the floor in that part of the house. Many of the floor joints had been removed.

Crash! Through the baby monitor Alex heard the sound of Jernigan crashing through the second floor.

Smash! Then through the first floor.

Crunk! He'd just landed in the basement. That would take care of him for a while.

Alex looked back at the TVs in time to see Alice take a running start at the back porch. That meant she'd noticed that the porch steps had been sawed.

By jumping over the sawed steps she would avoid *that* obvious booby trap.

Alice ran and jumped. She easily cleared the steps and landed on the porch itself. Where more boards had been sawed.

Ka-bong! A board flew up and smacked her in the back of the head.

"Help!" She screamed as she fell through the porch and into a stairwell leading down to the basement.

"Alice?" Through the baby monitor came the sound of Beaupre calling to her. If Beaupre was looking for her, he'd probably step up on the back porch, too.

Alex counted to himself. Three . . . two . . . one.

Ka-bong! Beaupre had just stepped onto the porch where a loose board flew up and smacked him in the face.

"Help!" And now Beaupre was joining Alice in a heap at the bottom of the stairwell.

Bang! Bang! Bang! Bang! The sound of rapidly fired shots rang through the house. Alex wondered what Beaupre was firing at now.

Grooof! Grooof! Ahhh-wooo! From all over the neighborhood came the sound of alarmed dogs barking at the sound of the shots. Alex thought it was rather inconsiderate of the burglars to disturb the neighbors.

Another crash meant that Unger had found his way to the basement also. Up in the attic, Alex nodded grimly. Things were going according to plan.

Brrrriiinnnggg! Suddenly, a phone started ringing somewhere downstairs. Alex caught his breath. *That* was definitely *not* part of the plan!

40

It was a really bad time to leave the attic, but Alex had no choice. He ran downstairs to his parents' room and grabbed the phone. "Hello?"

"Hi, hon, how's it going?" It was his mother.

"Everything's fine," Alex quickly replied. He could hear movement down in the basement. The burglars were probably getting ready for their next attack.

"The weather's terrible," his mom said. "It's snowing really hard. I was thinking of coming home as soon as I could."

"No!" Alex gasped a little too quickly. "Take your time. I'm, er, playing Chinese checkers with Mrs. Hess. She's creaming me."

He could hear the burglars coming up the basement steps. He couldn't let his mom come home now. The burglars might take her hostage or something. Then he'd have a *real* mess on his hands.

"Oh, I'm glad," his mother said. "I mean, not

that Mrs. Hess is creaming you. But that she's there."

Now Alex heard a new sound. It was closer. It sounded like the burglars were in the kitchen.

"Mom, I have to go," Alex said in a rush. "Mrs. Hess gets nutty when you make her wait."

He hung up the phone and ran into his room to get Doris. It was time to call out the reserves. Holding the white rat firmly in his hands, he snuck out into the second-floor hall.

He heard a louder creaking sound now. The burglars were coming up the steps from the first floor!

Alex quickly put Doris down in the hall. The rat scampered away toward the stairs.

Alex turned to run back upstairs. Wait! He couldn't! They'd hear him. He looked around desperately for a place to hide.

The burglars were nearly to the top of the stairs.

Alex pulled open a door. It was the linen closet, filled with towels and sheets. Not a real good hiding place. But he had no choice. He stepped in and quickly closed the door.

It was dark in the closet. Alex tried to stay perfectly still. Outside he could hear the creaking footsteps as the burglars reached the top of the stairs.

41

In the basement, Peter Beaupre had listened in on the kid's telephone conversation with his mother. As much as he wanted to kill the little worm, he had to admit he was pretty courageous for an eight-year-old.

Meanwhile on the second floor, Alice, Jernigan, and Unger had reached the top of the stairs.

"I'll go left," said Alice. "Mr. Unger goes right. Mr. Jernigan covers the stairs."

In the closet Alex noticed a button in the doorknob. It must have been the lock. He reached up and pressed it.

Click! Oh, no! The noise it made was too loud.

Outside in the hall Unger heard the noise. He knew exactly where it had come from. He grabbed the doorknob.

Inside the closet, Alex watched in terror as the doorknob jiggled. Someone on the other side was trying to get in.

They'd found him! Alex backed into the towels

and bit his lip in an effort not to cry out in fear.

The doorknob rattled and then stopped. Alex's heart was pounding so hard he could feel the blood thumping through his forehead. He could hardly breathe.

He heard a metallic squeak and a grunt.

"I'm coming to get you, shorty," a deep voice growled. "I'm coming to pay you back for all the misery you caused me."

It sounded like Unger. Alex looked around desperately for a place to hide. His eyes focused on a big fabric storage hanger hanging from the inside of the door. The pockets of it were filled with cleaning supplies, rags, and brushes.

Snap! The next thing he knew, the doorknob fell right off the door!

42

The door swung open. Unger stared in with a malicious smile as if he couldn't wait to turn Alex into chicken feed.

The smile faded. There was no trace of Alex. Unger scowled. It wasn't possible! He'd heard the lock click. Since when did doors lock by themselves?

Alice came up behind him with her gun drawn.

"So?" she asked.

"Towels," Unger replied with a shrug. He even turned on a closet light and looked around. "I don't get it. I saw this door close. I heard it lock."

Alice shook her head as if to imply that Unger was imagining things.

"Would I make it up?" Unger sputtered. "What's the point? It's not like we're working on commission here."

He closed the door.

Hanging between the fabric storage hanger and the door, Alex felt a wave of relief wash through him. He let go and dropped to the closet floor.

That was close. Way too close.

He pushed the linen door open just a little and peeked out. The hall was empty, but he decided to wait before he tried to get back to the attic.

43

Alice went back to her side of the second floor. She was disgusted. Unger was just an idiot imagining kids in linen closets. They'd be better off without him.

With Jernigan behind her, she came to a closed door. She glanced back at Jernigan. "Cover me," she whispered as she closed her hand on the door-knob and turned it.

Holding her gun high, Alice pushed the door open slowly and looked in. It was a girl's bed-room. The room was a mess. The floors were covered with clothes and magazines. Posters were falling off the walls.

Just then Alice caught a glimpse of movement out of the corner of her eye. There in the bed! Someone was sleeping!

Holding her gun out in front of her, Alice moved slowly toward the bed. She could barely see the person under all the blankets and clothes, but she could easily imagine that kid hiding there.

If he could set up all those booby traps, he could probably fire a gun, too.

Alice's finger closed nervously over the trigger of her gun.

She stepped closer.

Suddenly, the person in the bed moved.

44

*B*ang! *Bang! Bang!* The sound of rapidly fired bullets made Alex wince and duck. The sound had come from Molly's room. Alex had a feeling one of the burglars had just shot up Molly's other gorilla.

In Molly's room, Alice shoved her still smoking gun into her pocket. Whoever was in that bed had just bought a ticket to the big chat room in the sky. Alice noticed a field hockey stick in the corner and picked it up.

She hooked the end of the stick under the bedclothes and swept the blankets and extra clothes away.

Alice blinked. She was looking down at a big gorilla doll. That's what she'd just shot . . . a doll.

Behind her, Jernigan laughed.

Alice spun around, gritting her teeth angrily. "Shut up!" she yelled at him.

"You shot a doll," Jernigan chuckled.

Alice pointed down at a foot pump on the floor.

"The kid must have set this up. I stepped on the pump and it —"

Suddenly she froze with her mouth agape. She went white with terror.

Jernigan couldn't figure out what was wrong. Alice was staring at him, but why? All he was wearing was his torn camouflage outfit.

Squeak. . . . Something made a sound.

Jernigan looked down. Some kind of little animal had poked its head out of his camouflage suit. It looked like a little white . . . rat.

Uh-oh . . .

Jernigan looked back at Alice. She was holding the hockey stick like a baseball bat.

She started to swing.

"No —" Jernigan cried.

Too late.

45

In the linen closet, Alex heard a loud, anguished howl. Like a man was in horrible pain. Alex didn't know what that was, but with everyone screaming and howling, it seemed like a good time to get out of the closet and head back to the attic.

Unfortunately, it wasn't a good time.

No sooner did Alex leave the closet than Unger came out of his parents' room and saw him.

"The kid!" Unger shouted.

Alex leaped toward the stairs up to the attic, slammed the attic door behind him, and locked it. Doris scampered up the stairs beside him. The doorknob rattled as the burglars tried to get it open.

Alex knew he didn't have much time. He pulled on a backpack filled with supplies. Then he picked up Doris and the remote-controlled toy car.

Bang! Bang! More gunshots. Alex didn't have to guess what those were for. One of the burglars

121

had just shot off the doorknob. Now he heard the sound of their steps as they hurried up toward the attic.

Alex climbed into the dumbwaiter.

Then he reached out and pushed a button on the control panel on the wall.

The dumbwaiter started to go down. A second later, Alex was gone.

46

Down in the basement, Alex crawled out of the dumbwaiter. He pulled off the backpack and took out some tools. He used those tools to remove the floor of the dumbwaiter. Then he took a toy robot out of the backpack. It was battery-operated and had little mechanical arms that swung forward as it moved.

Alex set up the robot about four feet from the basement control panel for the dumbwaiter. Then he switched the robot on. The robot started to move slowly toward the control panel, swinging its arms as it went.

Next he crossed the basement to the washing machine. As part of his plan he'd left his hat and coat and Nerf dart gun there. He pulled on the hat and coat and picked up the dart gun.

Something was wrong. The gun weighed a ton! Alex looked down at it. His eyes went wide!

It wasn't the dart gun! It was a *real* gun!

One of the burglars must have left it. He

must've been so dazed from falling into the basement that he'd picked up the dart gun by accident.

Alex had no use for a real gun. He opened the trash can beside the washing machine and put it inside.

Then he let himself out of the basement and headed outside into the backyard. The snow was deep and soft. More of it was still falling from the sky. It would have been a lot of fun to make a new snow fort. Too bad he had to deal with these dumb burglars instead.

Alex positioned himself in the middle of the backyard where he could see the attic window. He crossed his fingers. If he was lucky, the best was yet to come.

47

Earl Unger couldn't believe what he was seeing. The attic looked like a command center. Granted it was filled with old junky TV sets, but they worked! On their screens he could see the driveway and backyard terrace.

"This is unbelievable," he groaned. "The kid was watching us the whole time! He had cameras on us!"

"I'll tell you what's *really* unbelievable," Jernigan said after searching the attic. "He's not here."

Unger looked up from the TV screens. "What do you mean, he's not here? Where could he be?"

At that very moment, a kid's voice came through the window shouting, "Hey! You're not going to find me up there, you big, dumb, law-breaking knuckleheads."

Alice, Unger, and Jernigan rushed to the window and looked out. Down on the snow-covered ground below, the kid was looking up at them with his hands cupped around his mouth.

"He's outside," Alice moaned.

Alex reached into his pocket and held up the Axus Defense microchip. "Looking for this?"

Three floors up, the burglars' jaws all dropped in unison.

Alex turned around and walked to the gate that led to the alley behind the house. He went through it and closed it behind him. Then he peeked through the fence.

The three burglars stood at the window, looking down in disbelief.

"How did he get outside?" Unger asked.

"The same way you're going to get outside," Alice informed him.

"How's that?" Jernigan asked.

"Jump," Alice said.

Jernigan stared at her like she'd lost her mind.

Alice pointed down. Below them on the ground was a trampoline.

"You're not serious," Unger said to her.

"If a kid can do it, *you* can do it," Alice replied with perfect seriousness.

"Children are more flexible," Unger said.

"It's a trampoline," Alice reminded him. "You're jumping into a *trampoline*."

"If we're going to be jumping into a trampoline," Jernigan said, "what will *you* be doing?"

Alice held up her gun. "I'll cover you."

48

A lex waited behind the fence.

Finally, Unger and Jernigan opened the third-floor window.

Alex smiled to himself. This wasn't going to be good.

It was going to be *spectacular*!

The two burglars jumped.

As they fell through the air, Alex watched them tense for the rebound off the trampoline.

The two burglars hit the trampoline.

Riiipppp! The two burglars went *through* the trampoline.

Shrraapp! The two burglars went through the pool cover.

Ker-plash! The two burglars smashed through the ice and disappeared into the pool.

Alex sighed. If only he'd had a video camera for *that*!

49

Up on the third floor, Alice watched Unger and Jernigan disappear through the trampoline. She had to admit that she wasn't entirely disappointed in the development.

Clunk! A sound from the other side of the attic caught her attention.

Behind the fence, Alex watched as Alice left the window. He imagined that by now the toy robot had hit the UP button on the dumbwaiter control panel, sending the dumbwaiter back up to the attic.

Of course, Alice thought as she walked toward the dumbwaiter. *This* was how the kid had gotten downstairs.

Well, what was good for the goose was good for the gander.

So she crawled into the dumbwaiter herself.

Only, the dumbwaiter no longer had a bottom.

"Ahhhhhhhhhhhhhhhhhhhh!" Alex could hear

her scream all the way from the alley behind the yard.

It was a long scream.

After all, it was four floors from the attic to the basement.

Thunk! The scream ended.

Out in the alley, Alex dusted off his hands. All in a day's work.

50

But neither the day nor the work was over. Alex cut through backyards and circled around to Mrs. Hess's house. He found her in the garage, tied to a chair, wearing only a thin sweater. That was crazy. It was freezing out. Her head was tilted forward and she wasn't moving. Alex was afraid she might have died from fright or the cold.

Alex took off his backpack and left it on the garage workbench with the toy car. He crouched down in front of the old lady. "Mrs. Hess?"

Mrs. Hess slowly opened her eyes.

Alex felt a wave of relief. "You're okay now," he said softly. "I'm here."

He took off his coat and draped it around her shoulders.

"Just give me a second," he said, going around behind her. "I'll untie you."

He was in the middle of untying her when he felt an uneasy sensation. He stopped and looked up.

But there was nothing there.

He started to untie her again, but as he did, he was overcome with a feeling of dread.

He looked up again.

Just as Peter Beaupre stepped out from behind Mrs. Hess's car.

Alex froze. Beaupre smiled.

"Well, son — it's Alex isn't it?" he said. "Today you learned a valuable lesson. There's a price to be paid for being a good citizen. In your zeal to rescue your neighbor, you finally stepped into one of *my* traps."

Alex swallowed and didn't reply. Beaupre went over to the workbench and picked up the toy car. He nearly ripped it apart with his hands, then tossed it aside when he saw that the chip wasn't there.

Next, he dumped the contents of the backpack on the workbench and started to go through them.

Alex cleared his throat. "Can Mrs. Hess go inside? She's very old and she's very cold."

Beaupre ignored him.

"Please?" Alex asked.

Beaupre didn't answer. The chip wasn't in the backpack either. Beaupre walked over to Alex and grabbed him by the collar, nearly lifting him off his feet.

"Give me the chip," Beaupre growled.

Alex shook his head. "It doesn't belong to you."

Beaupre reached into his pocket and pulled out a gun. He aimed it at Alex's face.

Trembling with fear, Alex stared down the barrel. He realized with a start that there was a dart in there. It wasn't a real gun. It was his Nerf dart gun.

"The chip, son," Beaupre said ominously. "Give me the chip or else."

Alex nodded at the gun. "That doesn't belong to you either."

Beaupre frowned. "What?"

"That isn't your gun," Alex said.

Beaupre looked at the gun. He pointed it at the ceiling and pulled the trigger.

A dart shot out and hit a support beam.

Alex reached into his coat pocket and took out another gun.

"*This* is your gun," he said.

Beaupre stared at it in disbelief.

Alex forced a confident smile on his face.

Peter Beaupre turned around and ran out of the garage as fast as he could.

Alex squeezed the trigger of the gun in his hand.

A stream of water bubbles came out.

51

Alex managed to get Mrs. Hess out of the garage and into her kitchen, where he helped her into a kitchen chair. The old lady wasn't shivering so much anymore, but she still looked pretty cold.

Alex pulled open the kitchen pantry doors. Inside was a row of canned soups.

"These are the times that call for soup," he said. "Got any favorites?"

"I'm fine, honey," Mrs. Hess replied. "Thanks anyway."

She was starting to get some color back in her face. Alex was impressed.

"Know what, Mrs. Hess?" he said. "It's really cold outside. You must be a pretty tough old bird."

"And you're a very sweet young man," Mrs. Hess replied. "I just never took the time to notice."

"You're not alone in that," Alex said, thinking of his brother and sister.

Outside came the loud grumble and scraping of a snowplow. Alex looked out Mrs. Hess's window and was shocked to see a bunch of police cars with their lights flashing. Next came some black cars and then came his mom's car.

"Gotta go, Mrs. Hess," Alex said, heading for her front door.

"Come back and visit," Mrs. Hess said with a wave.

Alex left the old lady's house. Down on the street, his mom was looking around with a really worried expression on her face.

Alex cupped his hands around his mouth and called, "Hey, Mom!"

Mrs. Pruitt spun around. Alex jogged toward her, but made the mistake of getting too close. The next thing he knew, she scooped him into her arms and started hugging and kissing him. Meanwhile, the police were all over the place.

"Mom?" Alex started to squirm out of her grasp. "You're hugging and kissing me in front of the cops."

"I'm so sorry," Mrs. Pruitt said as she put him down. "I'm so sorry I didn't listen to you about those burglars."

Stan came up and offered his hand. Alex shook it.

"This is very cool," Stan said.

"You're a hero," Molly said, patting him on the shoulder.

A man wearing a long, dark coat came up to them. "Alex Pruitt?"

"That's me," Alex said.

The man took out an identification card. "I'm Agent Stuckey with the FBI, son. I think you have something we've been looking for."

"Here." Alex reached into his pocket and handed Stuckey the Axus Defense microchip. "Also, there's a senior citizen across the street who needs some soup and a doctor's care. And there are two burglars in the pool and a third one in our basement. But the other guy got away."

Agent Stuckey reached into his pocket and took out a photograph of Peter Beaupre. "Is this him?"

Alex looked at the photograph and nodded.

"We've been after him for seven years," Stuckey said. "But somehow he always manages to slip away."

52

Peter Beaupre's butt was freezing. He was sit-ting on the icy ground in the kid's snow fort behind the house. It was just the sort of place the cops would never bother to check. If he could manage to sit there until dark, he was pretty sure he could escape. Beaupre had to smile to himself. The FBI would really kick themselves if he got away again.

Suddenly he heard the flutter of wings. Some kind of bird landed in the entrance to the snow fort. It was all green, with a big hooked beak and long green tail feathers.

A parrot! Beaupre realized. What in the world was a parrot doing there?

"Awk," the parrot called softly, then began to sing that old song, "Bad, Bad Leroy Brown."

It sounded familiar. . . . Beaupre knew he'd heard it recently. But where?

The phone machine in the Alcotts' house!

Beaupre stared at the parrot in shock. Meanwhile, the dumb bird was still singing. If the cops heard it, they might check the snow fort and catch him.

Beaupre pressed his finger to his lips. He had to shut the dumb bird up!

But the bird kept right on singing.

Desperate, Beaupre reached into his pocket and came up with a cellophane-wrapped cracker from the San Francisco-Chicago flight. He quickly unwrapped the cracker and held it out. The parrot studied the cracker, then hopped closer. It reached out with a claw and grabbed it.

Beaupre felt a wave of relief as the bird ate the cracker.

Then the bird cocked its head and gave Beaupre a questioning look.

At first the burglar didn't understand. Then the parrot raised its claw. It wanted another cracker.

"I . . . I only had one," Beaupre stammered.

The parrot studied the burglar for a second, then shook its head. "Say good night, Gracie."

Beaupre lunged. The parrot jumped away.

"Emergency!" the dumb bird squawked loudly. *"Calling all cars! Intruder!"*

Beaupre lunged again, this time landing outside the fort.

Again he missed the bird.

He looked up. Right into the barrel of a police officer's gun. The police officer smiled. "Looks like the bird got away," he said. "Looks like this time you won't."

53

The bad guys were taken away. Unger and Jernigan walked stiffly in their frozen pants. The police had to carry Alice away because she was sort of permanently scrunched up from her fall down the dumbwaiter shaft. Peter Beaupre just kept muttering, "Polly want a cracker?" over and over.

The police and the FBI were so thankful that Alex had helped catch the bad guys that they arranged for workers to come in and fix all the damage in the house. While they patched, painted, and cleaned, Mrs. Pruitt ordered a bunch of pizzas for her family and Mrs. Hess and the FBI and Chief of Police Flanagan.

A little while later they all sat around the kitchen table eating the pizza and talking about dumb family stuff. Alex could tell that his mom still felt guilty about leaving him in the house alone.

"Hey, listen," Agent Stuckey said as he chewed

on a piece of pizza. "Child care's a rough deal. I know. My wife works."

"Mine, too," said the other FBI agent, a guy named Rogers.

"I'm home all day, every day," Mrs. Hess chimed in. "If you need a hand, all you need to do is call."

"Do you have any plans for tomorrow?" Alex asked her.

"Just to watch the soaps," Mrs. Hess replied.

"Have you had the chicken pox?" asked Alex.

"Honey, I had the chicken pox when Herbert Hoover was in the White House," she said.

Mrs. Hess wouldn't have to worry about catching chicken pox from Alex — the way every one of the crooks had!

The front door opened and Mr. Pruitt came in, carrying his overnight bag. He looked surprised at all the activity, but when he saw Alex, he smiled.

Alex ran to him. Mr. Pruitt picked him up and hugged him. "I heard all about what happened. You sure don't look any worse for the wear."

"They couldn't touch me," Alex replied with a wink.

The FBI agents and the chief of police stood up and introduced themselves. Mr. Pruitt kept looking around at all the workers with an amazed expression on his face.

"Axus Technologies is giving Alex a reward for

getting their stolen microchip back," Stan said.

"It's a large six-figure sum," Molly added. "Which is extremely nice of them."

"And the city sent over a crew to fix the place up," Mrs. Pruitt said.

"I can see," Mr. Pruitt said with a nod.

Just then, a paramedic came into the kitchen carrying the gorilla doll Alice had shot up. The paramedic had bandaged the gorilla's bullet holes.

"Gee, thanks," Molly said, taking the gorilla and setting it beside her.

"Well, I think we've learned a lot from this," said Chief Flanagan. "Most importantly, I think we learned something about listening to our kids."

Everyone nodded in agreement.

"We know now that if you come to us with something you think isn't right, we're obliged to check it out," said Mr. Pruitt.

"Good," said Alex. "And by the way, did you bring me anything from your trip?"

"I sure did," Mr. Pruitt said. He reached into his bag and pulled out a box . . . with a picture of a toy car on it.

The same toy car that had caused all the trouble in the first place.

Alex took the box and smiled. "Thanks, Dad. It's just what I always wanted."

About the Author

Todd Strasser has written many award-winning novels for young and teenage readers. Among his best-known books are *Help! I'm Trapped in Obedience School* and *Girl Gives Birth to Own Prom Date*. He speaks frequently at schools about the craft of writing and conducts writing workshops for young people. He and his family live outside New York City with their yellow Labrador retreiver, Mac. His most recent project for Scholastic was a series about Camp Run-a-Muck.